A tale of a girl who is both black and white

Written by Tiffany Catledge
Illustrated by Anissa Riviére

ISBN: 1481899023
ISBN 13: 9781481899024
Library of Congress Control Number: 2013900165
CreateSpace Independent Publishing Platform
North Charleston, South Carolina

Little Mixie wonders why everyone wants to know WHAT she is.

Isn't it obvious?
She is clearly a human being.

And anyway, isn't WHO she is what matters most?

Coming from a family with a black dad and a white mom makes her extra special, and maybe a little different too.
But different is good.
Mixie embraces her uniqueness and determines to be the best "Me" she can be.

Dedication:

To my parents Art & Judy Harding
Who were pioneers in mixing the world!

with love
Tiffany

Someone Called me an
Oreo Cookie®.
Chocolate on the outside,
vanilla in the middle.

I don't feel like a cookie.

I feel like me!

Mixed Me.

When God made me He took some of my vanilla mom and my chocolate dad

and started to mix.

He mixed

and mixed. . .

and mixed!

He popped me in the oven
and out I came- Mixed Me!

Cooked to the perfect me!

Just as you are the perfect mix of you!

Once, I hurt myself at the playground and a boy asked, "why is your blood RED? I thought it would be GREEN!"

I may be a different MIX than you,
but my blood is red, just like yours.
Just like you, it hurts when I get a scrape.

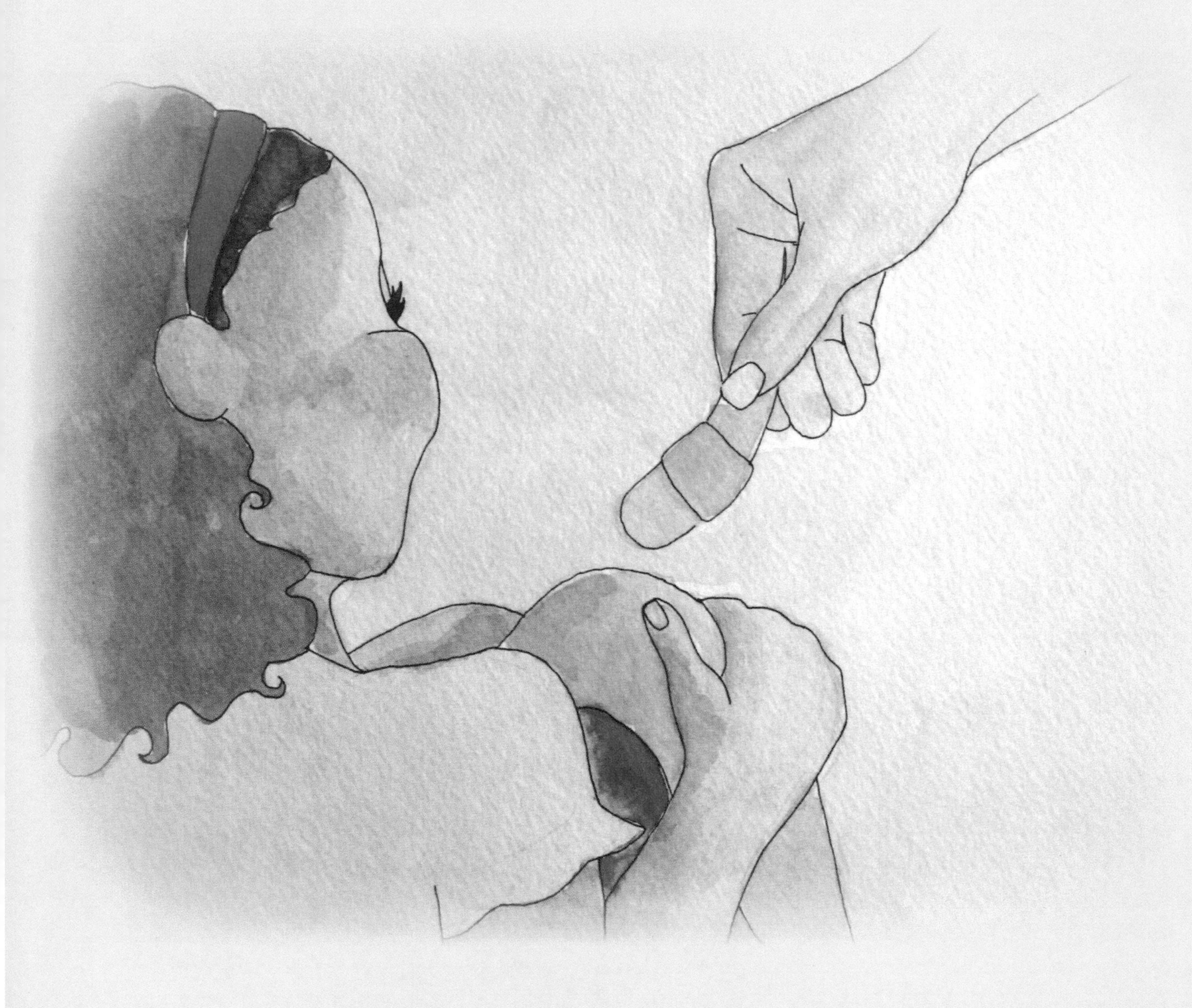

People sometimes ask me,

"What are you?"

I think that is a funny question because I am most obviously a human being!

And anyway,

it is not WHAT I am,
but WHO.

Being the best me I can be
is what matters most.

People don't always believe that
my mom is my mom because
her skin is different from mine.

But she is. She is mine and I am hers.

I am often asked, "Where do you belong?
In this group or that group?"

Since I am both
I belong in both.

Right in the
middle.

And remember,
it is not WHAT I am, but WHO.
Being the best me I can be
is what matters most.

When I look in the mirror,
what do I see?

I see someone unique,
someone special,
someone made with the
perfect blend of black and white.

I see me. . . Mixed Me

I am me. MIXED ME.
And I am beautiful!
It does not matter
WHAT I am, but WHO.
Being the best ME I can be
is what matters most.

No matter how you were made . . .
a mix of

black, brown,

white or yellow,

red, pink or olive

you are unique
you are special
you are beautiful!

Who are you?

Draw YOU, right here in the book!

Be the best YOU, you can be!

About the Author

Tiffany Catledge lives in Southern California. This is her first book in a planned *Mixed Me* series. She is married, and she and her husband have six glorious children, all a wonderful mix! She is the daughter of Art & Judy and sibling to four mixed sisters and brothers. She received her Bachelor's Degree in Intercultural Communication from Arizona State University, and has always been interested in cultures, ethnicities, and of course MIXES! In her free time she enjoys reading and being with her family. One of her favorite hangouts is the children's section of her local library.

To learn more, please visit her at:
www.mixedme.org

and like her Facebook page:
www.facebook.com/mixedmom

About the Illustrator

Anissa Rivière is seventeen years old and lives in San Diego, California. She attends Del Norte High School, and was recently accepted to the prestigious Rhode Island School of Design. She has always loved art of any kind, especially drawing and painting. She lives with her Jamaican father, Caucasian mother, and curly-haired little sister. She hopes to become a product designer, and to illustrate more books in the future. She loves her mixed background and wouldn't want it any other way!

25568224R00021

Made in the USA
Lexington, KY
28 August 2013